The Daydreamer

Retold by Kate Davies

Illustrated by Kate Sheppard

Reading consultant: Alison Kelly
Roehampton University

Daisy has no money.
"Take my milk
to market," says
the farmer.

3

"Yes!" says Daisy.

And she sets off for the market.

Market this way

"Soon I'll have some money," she thinks.

Market

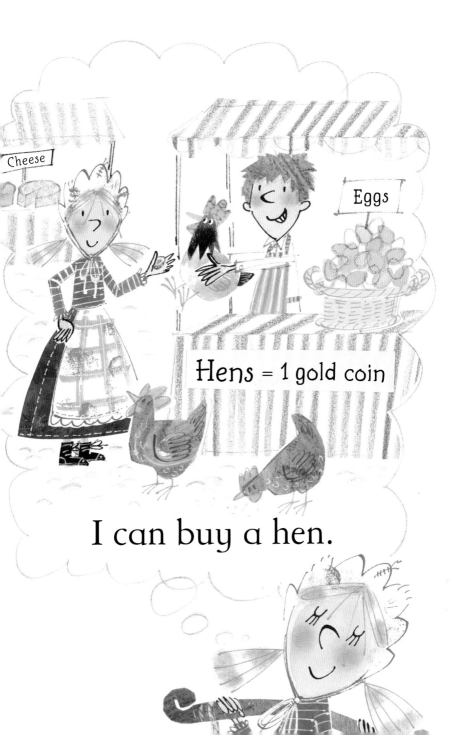

Cheese

Eggs

Hens = 1 gold coin

I can buy a hen.

My hen will lay eggs...

...lots of
eggs.

I can sell my eggs.

Best eggs in all
the land!

I'll buy a pretty dress...

...and sparkly shoes.

But I won't get
dressed by myself.

I'll have servants to help me!

I'll marry a prince.

I'll be a princess.

We'll live in a palace...

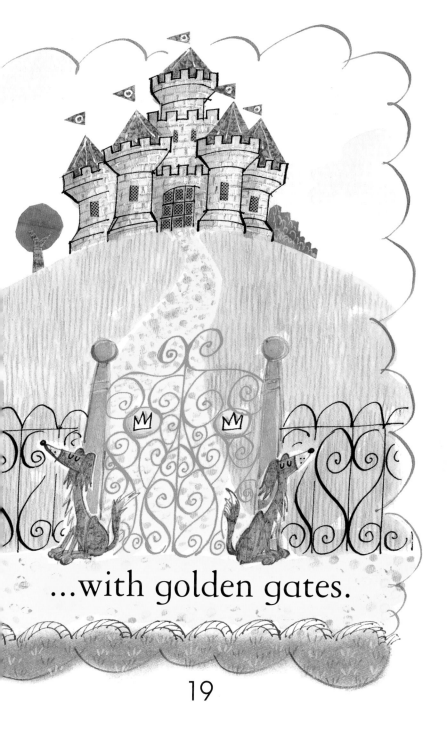

...with golden gates.

We'll have a ball.

I'll twirl and whirl in my
new dress.

SPLISH!

SPLASH!

SPLOSH!

The milk is gone!
Poor Daisy.

Cheer up!
There's no use crying
over spilt milk.

Puzzles

Puzzle 1

Can you spot the differences
between the two pictures?

There are
six to find.

Puzzle 2
Match the words to the picture.

palace

pony

prince

26

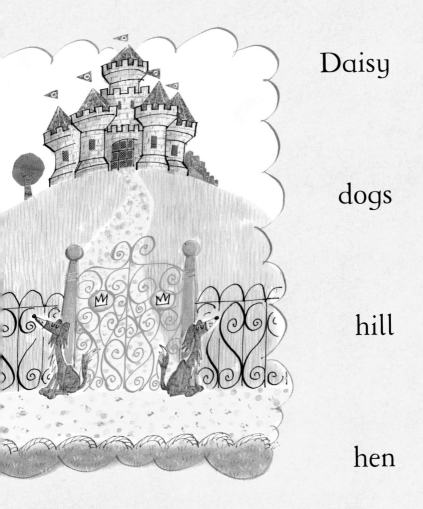

Daisy

dogs

hill

hen

27

Puzzle 3

Choose the best speech bubble for each picture.

29

Answers to puzzles

Puzzle 1

Puzzle 2

palace

hill

prince

Daisy

dogs

hen

pony

Puzzle 3

"There are lots of eggs!"

"We're dancing."

"I can buy a hen."

About
The Daydreamer

The Daydreamer is one of Aesop's Fables, a collection of stories first told in Ancient Greece. Today, different versions of the story are told all around the world. In India, the daydreamer is a poor man who dreams of selling his last bowl of food. In Russia, the daydreamer is a thief who dreams of selling stolen cucumbers.

Designed by Lisa Verrall
Series editor: Lesley Sims
Series designer: Russell Punter

First published in 2010 by Usborne Publishing Ltd., Usborne House,
83-85 Saffron Hill, London EC1N 8RT, England. www.usborne.com
Copyright © 2010 Usborne Publishing Ltd.